The Three Grasshoppers

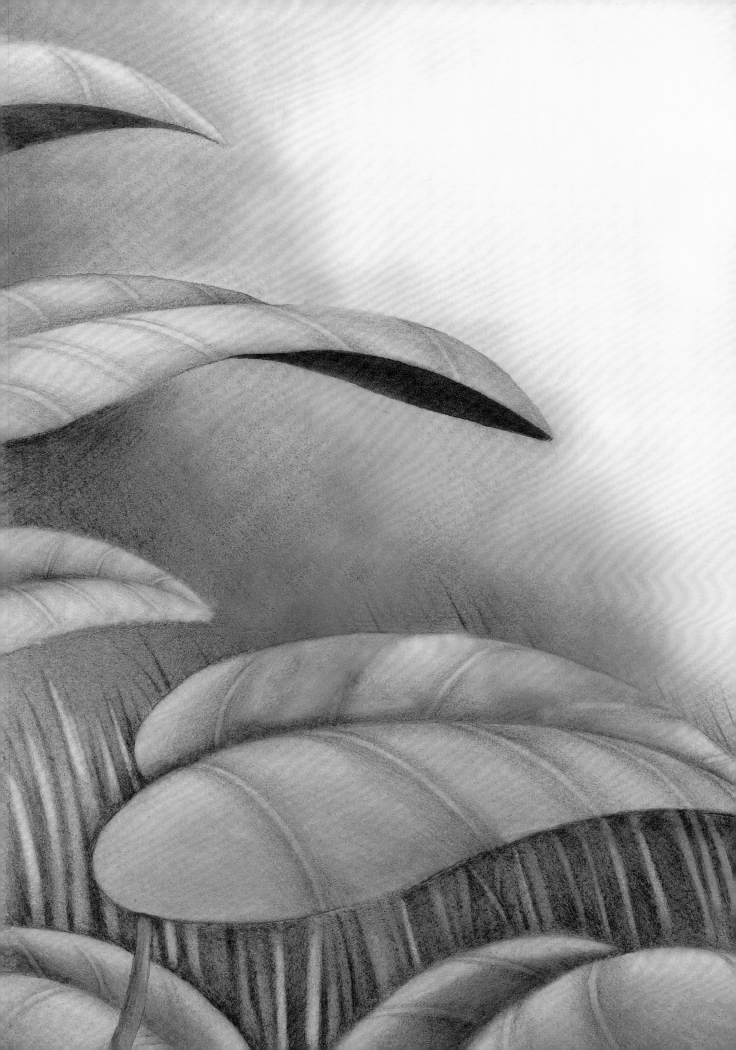

The Three Grasshoppers

By **Francesca Bosca**

Illustrated by **Giuliano Ferri**

Purple Bear Books
New York

Once upon a time there were three grasshoppers, Charlie, Connor, and Carl, who were best friends and talented musicians.

Every night they would gather in a corner
of the field singing and playing their instruments,
making wonderful music together. They wrote songs
together, too, and when the other grasshoppers heard
them, they would join in singing.

One night Connor turned to his friends. "I'm hungry," he said. "Is there anything to eat?"

Charlie, the oldest of the three, replied, "Oh, dear. We have eaten almost all of our food. This isn't good. Winter is coming and we don't want to end up like the famous singing grasshopper."

"What famous singing grasshopper?" asked Carl.

"Why, she is a grasshopper legend!" Charlie replied. "It's said that she so loved to sing that she spent the entire summer doing nothing but singing and had nothing to eat when winter came. Starving, she asked the ants for help, but they refused. 'Since you spent all summer singing,' they told her, 'you should be able to survive the winter by dancing.'"

"That's a terrible story!" said Carl.

Charlie and Connor nodded.

"We'd better do something so we don't end up like that poor singing grasshopper!" they all agreed.

Connor had an idea. "The ants are hard workers," he said. "Let's learn from them."

So the three grasshoppers observed the ants, studying and recording their every move. And then they went to work themselves.

But before long, the three friends began to argue and complain about each other. Charlie was too bossy. Connor was always taking rests. And the youngest, Carl, was too slow.

Things went from bad to worse, and soon all three grasshoppers decided they would be better off working alone. Each built his own storage bin in a clearing in the field and raced around gathering food to fill it.

The three grasshoppers worked harder and harder—day and night they worked. When their storage bins were full, they built new ones and kept on working. They were so busy, they didn't have time to speak to each other or to make music together in the evenings.

The other grasshoppers missed hearing the three friends' music. Some of them went to see what had happened. They met Charlie hurrying along with a jug of sap. "We can't sing anymore or we won't have anything to eat for the winter," he told them. "You'd better get to work, too, or you'll surely starve!"

The grasshoppers were panicked by Charlie's warning.

"Don't worry," he reassured them. "It's not too late. I can guarantee you'll have plenty to eat all winter long—but only if you work for me!"

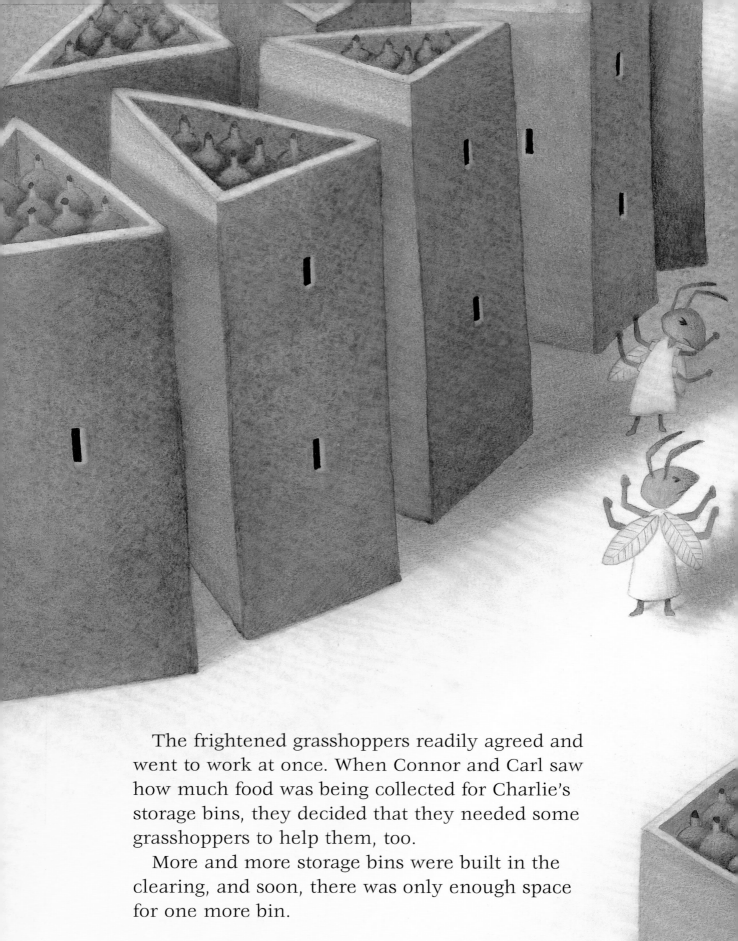

The frightened grasshoppers readily agreed and went to work at once. When Connor and Carl saw how much food was being collected for Charlie's storage bins, they decided that they needed some grasshoppers to help them, too.

More and more storage bins were built in the clearing, and soon, there was only enough space for one more bin.

All three groups of grasshoppers desperately wanted that last space and started fighting over it. They shouted so loudly and charged so fiercely that nobody noticed the large dark shadow moving closer and closer.

At the height of the battle, someone suddenly cried, "Elephant! Watch out for the elephant!"

The grasshoppers watched in horror as the huge elephant lumbered toward them—heading straight for their storage bins.

Closer and closer came the elephant, his gigantic
feet looming above them, threatening to crush the
grasshoppers and destroy all
their hard work. Terrified,
they fled, screaming and
beating their wings in panic.

Just as the elephant lifted his foot for what would surely be the fatal blow, Carl leaped onto a nearby blade of grass and started to sing as loud as he could. As he sang, he motioned to Charlie and Connor to join in.

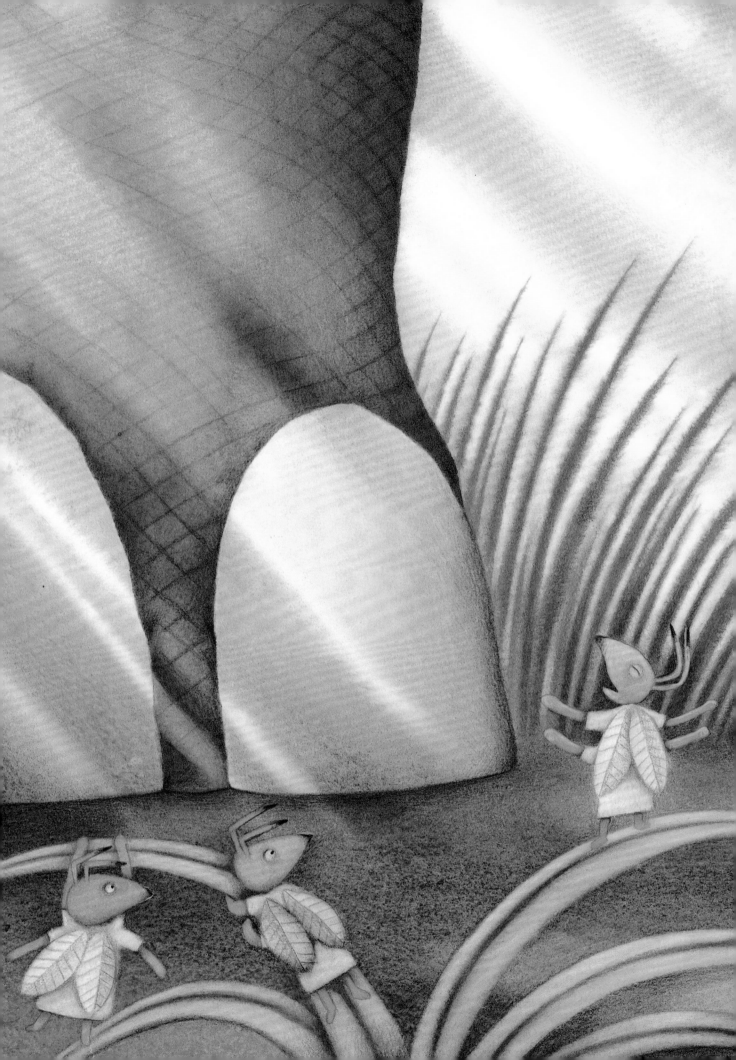

Uncertain what Carl was trying to do, Charlie and Connor whipped out their instruments and started playing anyway.

The elephant, fascinated, gently lowered his gigantic foot, just missing the storage bins. He turned to see where the music was coming from. The three grasshoppers continued playing and singing even louder, flying from stalk to stalk, and the elephant followed.

The plan worked! Together the three friends saved the day! The other grasshoppers cheered. They were safe, and they would all have food for the winter.

That night the three grasshoppers held a concert. Everyone celebrated, dancing and singing from atop the sunflowers. Happiest of all were Charlie, Connor, and Carl. They sang with pride and delight. They sang to celebrate their friendship, and they promised that from then on, they would always work and make music together.

Text copyright © 2004 by Francesca Bosca

Illustrations copyright © 2004 by Giuliano Ferri

First published in Taiwan in 2004 by Grimm Press

First English-language edition published in 2006 by Purple Bear Books Inc., New York.

For more information about our books, visit our website: purplebearbooks.com

Library of Congress Cataloging-in-Publication Data is available.

This edition prepared by Cheshire Studio.

Trade edition

ISBN-10: 1-933327-13-8

ISBN-13: 978-1-933327-13-6

1 3 5 7 9 TE 10 8 6 4 2

Library edition

ISBN-10: 1-933327-14-6

ISBN-13: 978-1-933327-14-3

1 3 5 7 9 LE 10 8 6 4 2

Printed in Taiwan